www.enchantedlionbooks.com

First American Edition published in 2015 by Enchanted Lion Books, 351 Van Brunt Street, Brooklyn, NY 11231
English language translation copyright © 2015 by Lyn Miller-Lachmann
English-language edition copyright © 2015 by Enchanted Lion Books
Originally published in Portugal by Planeta Tangerina © 2008 as *O mundo num segundo*
All rights reserved under International and Pan-American Copyright Conventions
A CIP record is on file with the Library of Congress
ISBN: 978-1-59270-157-5
Printed in Portugal on FSC paper from sustainable forests

First Printing

The publication of this book has been funded by the General Directorate for Books,
Archives and Libraries in Portugal.

GOVERNO DE
PORTUGAL

SECRETÁRIO DE ESTADO
DA CULTURA

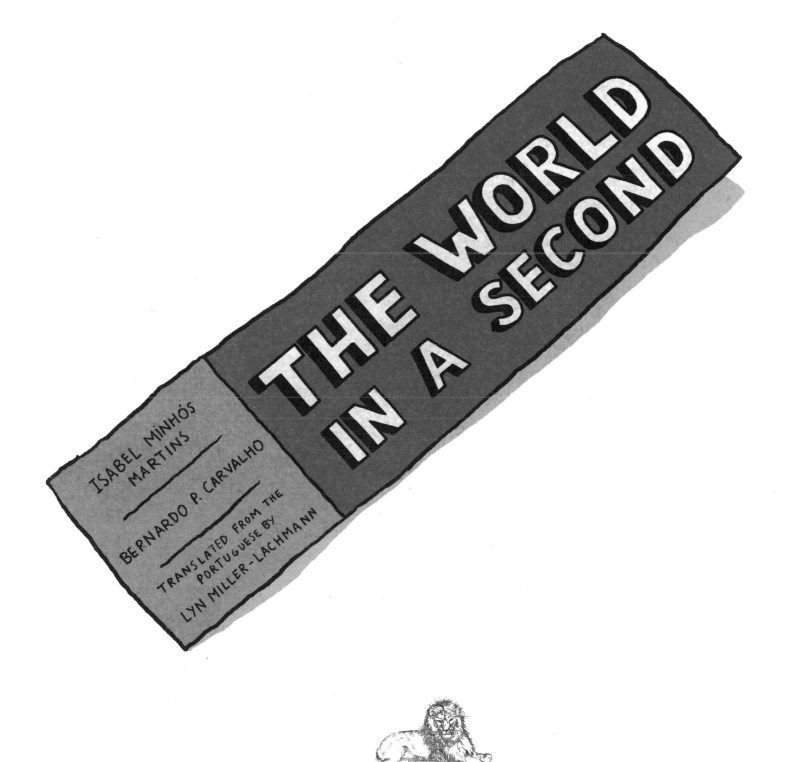

THE WORLD IN A SECOND

ISABEL MINHÓS MARTINS

BERNARDO P. CARVALHO

TRANSLATED FROM THE PORTUGUESE BY
LYN MILLER-LACHMANN

ENCHANTED LION BOOKS
NEW YORK

Every time a second crosses the world
(always running, always in a hurry),
millions of things happen,
here, there, everywhere...

While you turn the pages of this book,
the world doesn't stop...

... A boat is surprised by a storm on the Baltic Sea.

... On the other side of the world,

a volcano rumbles, then erupts.

... In a darkened room, a very old woman closes her eyes to sleep.

... A boy balances himself on his bicycle for the first time.

(Will he fall down one second later?)

... In an island barbershop,

a man bids farewell to his mustache.

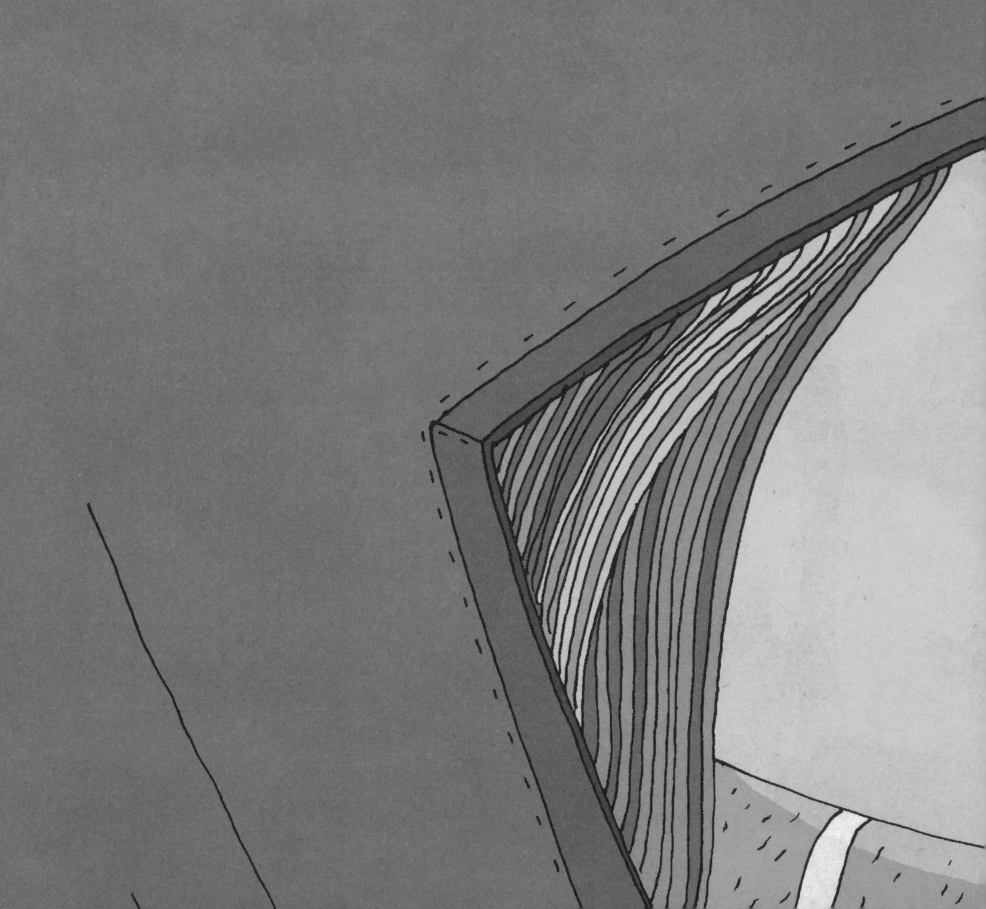

... A girl hurries home from school.

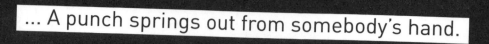

... In a Portuguese orchard, a ripe orange falls.

... Time seems to stop in a Moroccan village.

... After many days,

a breeze finally flutters on the high seas.

1 Buenos Aires, Argentina, 9:32 am

2 Baltic Sea, 2:32 pm

3 New York, USA, 8:32 am

4 Guadalajara, Mexico, 7:32 am

5 Lae, Papua-New Guinea, 10:32 pm

6 Cartaxo, Portugal, 1:32 pm

7 Xangongo, Angola, 1:32 pm

8 Karabuk, Turkey, 3:32 pm

9 Velas, São Jorge, Azores, 12:32 am

10 Khalkis, Greece, 3:32 pm

11 Omsk, Russia, 7:32 pm

12 Seydisfjordur, Iceland, 12:32 pm

13 Tokyo, Japan, 9:32 pm

14 Sydney, Australia, 10:32 pm

15 Mértola, Portugal, 1:32 pm

16 Toubkal, Morocco, 12:32 pm

17 Coro, Venezuela, 8:02 am

18 Indian Ocean, 5:32 pm

19 Miskolc, Hungary, 2:32 pm

20 Pescara, Italy, 2:32 pm

21 Chicago, USA, 7:32 am

22 East London, South Africa, 2:32 pm

23 Florianópolis, Brazil, 9:32 am

Note: The time markings fall during spring in the northern hemisphere and include daylight savings time.